Aristocats

Madame de Bonnefamille was one of the most elegant
ladies who lived in Paris. She was the proud owner of a
most elegant white persian cat called Duchess, who had
three kittens, Berlioz, Toulouse and Marie. They were all so
elegant together that they were called the aristocats.

Every morning Madame de Bonnefamille would take
Duchess and the kittens for a trip in her carriage around
the Bois de Boulogne, the most elegant park in Paris.
Froufrou, the horse that pulled the carriage, loved these
daily walks, but Edgar, the butler, thought it was all rather
boring.

You see, Edgar could never understand why Madame de Bonnefamille paid so much attention to the aristocats – the four horrible creatures, as he called them – that caused so much havoc in the house.

Of course, he didn't understand, as Madame de Bonnefamille understood, that Duchess's kittens were all very artistic.

Berlioz was very musical, Toulouse loved painting pictures, and Marie had a fine singing voice.

For Madame de Bonnefamille, who was herself as artistic as she was elegant, the kittens were her pride and joy.

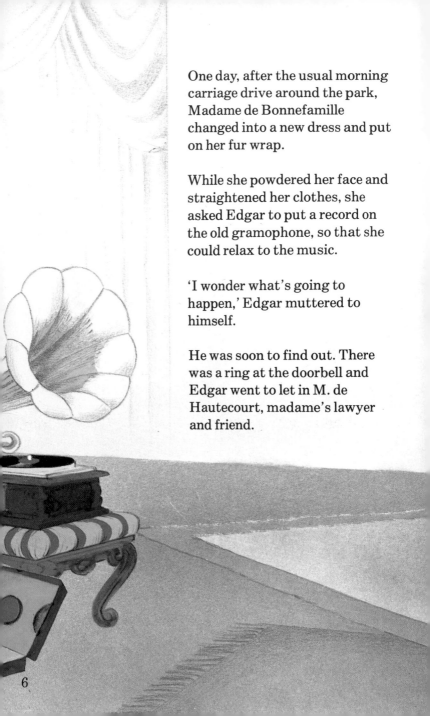

One day, after the usual morning carriage drive around the park, Madame de Bonnefamille changed into a new dress and put on her fur wrap.

While she powdered her face and straightened her clothes, she asked Edgar to put a record on the old gramophone, so that she could relax to the music.

'I wonder what's going to happen,' Edgar muttered to himself.

He was soon to find out. There was a ring at the doorbell and Edgar went to let in M. de Hautecourt, madame's lawyer and friend.

'M. de Hautecourt!' announced Edgar solemnly.

Madame de Bonnefamille took a last look at herself in the mirror, picked up Duchess and went to greet her most elegant lawyer.

'Delighted to see you, madame!' said M. de Hautecourt. And, most elegantly, he kissed her hand – or what he thought was her hand.

Actually, he kissed Duchess' tail by mistake. She was very surprised, but Madame de Bonnefamille was used to her lawyer's ways, and laughed to herself.

Edgar, who by now was more curious than ever to know what was going to happen, opened the lid of the speaking tube through which he could hear the conversation between M. de Hautecourt and Madame de Bonnefamille in the living room.

This is what he heard madame tell her lawyer:

'Because I have no one to whom I can leave my money when I die, I want to make a will leaving everything to my cats.

'I want my will to say that Edgar must continue to look after Duchess and her family of kittens and that he must give them everything they need to continue to practise their art.'

M. de Hautecourt said: 'Your decision does you great credit, madame.'

Edgar was furious. He jumped up and down in a terrible rage.

'Never, never, never!' he shouted out loud, even though no one could hear him. 'I'll get rid of those wretched cats right away – and then she'll have no one to leave her money to but *me*!'

He went off to the kitchen and began to prepare the cats' lunch, just as he always did.

Some bread, some milk, some honey . . . and today, something else!

Edgar poured ten pills into the cats' lunch-time drink.
'This will put them to sleep for a very long time!' he chuckled.

12

Lap, lap, lap!

Four pink tongues were soon greedily drinking at their bowls of milk.

Four?

Well, *five* really!

The fifth one, who had just arrived, belonged to Roquefort, a mouse, who was a good friend of Duchess and her kittens.

When Roquefort felt lonely he often popped out of his hole and joined the aristocats at their lunch.

Roquefort liked to dip a biscuit in the milk. That made it nice and soft to eat.

'Oh dear!' said Duchess, when she had finished her milk. 'I feel so tired.'

'So do we!' chorused Berlioz, Toulouse and Marie together.

Roquefort yawned. He just had time to get back to his hole before he fell asleep.

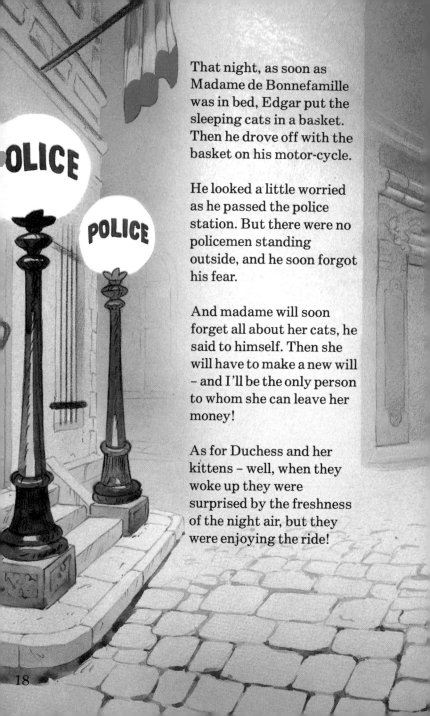

That night, as soon as Madame de Bonnefamille was in bed, Edgar put the sleeping cats in a basket. Then he drove off with the basket on his motor-cycle.

He looked a little worried as he passed the police station. But there were no policemen standing outside, and he soon forgot his fear.

And madame will soon forget all about her cats, he said to himself. Then she will have to make a new will – and I'll be the only person to whom she can leave her money!

As for Duchess and her kittens – well, when they woke up they were surprised by the freshness of the night air, but they were enjoying the ride!

At least they were enjoying it until Edgar, frightened by two barking dogs, swerved off the road and down a river bank.

Bomp, bomp, bomp! went his motor-cycle as it crashed down the bank.

The two dogs leaned over a brick wall as the motor-cycle came to a juddering halt against a rock.

As for the bag full of cats, it flew into the air . . .

. . . and landed under a
stone bridge by the
river.

Edgar didn't wait to
see how the aristocats
were. He pushed his
motor-cycle up the
river bank and sped
off into the night.

At dawn the next day
the cats woke up.

'Where are we?' cried
Berlioz.

'What's happened?'
cried Toulouse.

'Where is our
mistress?' cried
Marie.

'Calm down, children,'
said Duchess. 'I don't
know where we are or
what has happened,
but I must have a
moment to think
about our situation.'

24

That night Roquefort the mouse slept badly. He woke up in the middle of the night and strained his ears.

Not a sound from the house came back to him.

Roquefort knew there was something wrong, because he could always hear the cats breathing in the darkness when he woke up.

He crept quietly out of his hole into the kitchen. He called out, scratched at doors, climbed up on chairs.

But there was no sign of the cats. And even Edgar was missing from his bed.

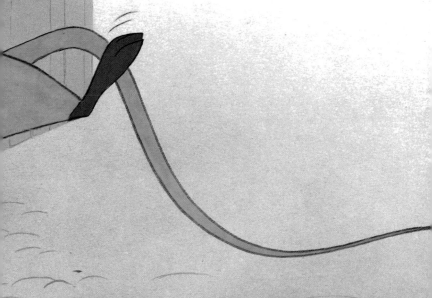

Miaow!

Duchess, deep in thought on the river bank, looked up in surprise.

Standing before her was a big, handsome brown and white cat.

'Madam,' he said. 'Allow me to introduce myself. I'm Thomas O'Malley, known as O'Malley the alley cat. You seem as if you may be in trouble. Is there any way in which I can help?'

Duchess smiled gratefully, and told O'Malley how she and her children had come to be on the river bank.

'Well, I'm just a tramp, you know,' said O'Malley when she had finished her story. 'But I'll sure do everything I can to help you, Princess.'

Princess! Duchess's eyes shone. At least O'Malley could see that she and her family were aristocats!

Marie, however, pulled a face. What does mama think she's doing, she said to herself, talking to the first stranger who happens to pass by?

Duchess, though, only wanted to get back to Paris safely with her family, and she told O'Malley just that.

The alley cat led them to a railway line. 'We'll follow these rails and they'll take us right back into Paris,' he said. 'Let's all sing a song as we march along!'

The kittens began to think that O'Malley was a rather nice cat.

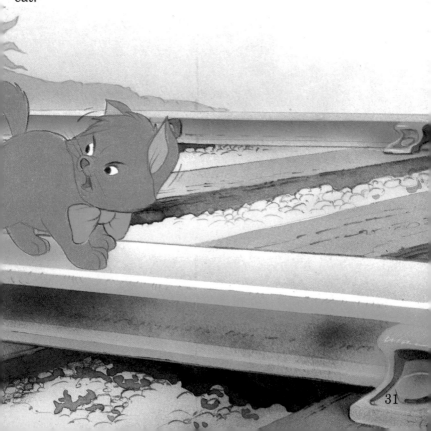

They marched all day and when night came they reached the edge of Paris. O'Malley took them on lots of short cuts over the rooftops.

Poor Marie! She was feeling quite exhausted. But she cheered up when O'Malley put her on his back and carried her along with him.

As they were crossing one rooftop they came to an open skylight, through which came the sound of loud music.

Peering down, they saw an orchestra of cats merrily playing.

'It's all right!' O'Malley shouted above the deafening noise. 'These are all friends of mine. And they're real cool cats!'

Berlioz, Toulouse and Marie peered through the open skylight in amazement. They had never seen such a sight or heard such a noise!

'My goodness, it's just like the opera!' gasped Marie, who always wanted to be a singer.

'I'm not sure it's quite like that, dear,' Duchess murmured thoughtfully. She wasn't at all sure that she liked *this* kind of music.

But O'Malley clearly loved it. He beat his front paw energetically in time to the music.

'It's called jazz,' he explained. 'See the cat with the trumpet? He's my old friend Luke Allstrong.'

The kittens clapped the trumpeter. 'Well played Luke Allstrong!' they shouted.

Well, if Madame de Bonnefamille, with her trained musical ear, could have seen what happened next!

Duchess, O'Malley and the kittens jumped through the skylight, and Duchess and O'Malley began to jive!

Perched on top of an old straw hat, Berlioz and Toulouse began to rock and roll in time to the music.

'Until this moment I always thought I was destined to be a classical musician,' said Berlioz. 'But now I can see a whole new musical future opening up before me.'

As for Marie, you can guess what she was doing. She climbed up on to the piano and began to sing at the top of her voice.

The sounds of joyful music drifted up through the open skylight and across the Paris rooftops.

Duchess was in an ecstasy as she danced and danced the night away.

Thomas O'Malley, she thought to herself, was the most wonderful cat she had ever met.

As the dawn came up over Paris, one by one the exhausted musicians fell asleep over their instruments.

The three kittens crept out on to the roof and there, to their amazement, they saw their mother sitting on a chimney pot with O'Malley the alley cat.

Duchess looked round and saw them at the same time.

'Good heavens,' she said. 'We must be on our way. Whatever will Madame de Bonnefamille be thinking now?'

'Oh, please stay a little longer, Princess,' sighed O'Malley. 'You really are such a wonderful lady!'

Duchess sighed, too. 'No, we really must be going,' she said.

'Then I'm coming with you!' cried O'Malley.

When Edgar returned to Madame de
Bonnefamille's house, madame was
out in the city, searching for her
beloved cats.

Edgar made himself comfortable.

'One day, when I've inherited all her
money, I'll be rich,' he said. 'So I'd
better get used to the feeling.'

Roquefort the mouse overheard all
this, and he quickly guessed what
Edgar had done. Angrily, he put on
his detective's hat and he, too, went
out to look for the cats.

44

No sooner had the mouse gone than Edgar heard a knock at the front door.

'Goodness me, madame must be back already!' he said. 'I must hide the cigars and champagne, quickly!'

He went to the front door. There on the doorstep were the aristocats. How could they have found their way home?

Then Edgar saw O'Malley. That alley cat must have shown them the way, he thought in dismay.

Edgar kicked O'Malley off the doorstep. He led the
aristocats indoors and took a big bag sack which he
plunged down over their heads.

The kittens cried out in terror. Their nightmare had begun
all over again.

'I'm frightened, mama!' cried Marie when they felt the
sack being lifted up and carried.

'Don't cry, children,' Duchess said anxiously. 'I'm sure
O'Malley will hear what has happened and then he will
rescue us.'

Duchess wasn't feeling very confident, but she knew she had to reassure the kittens.

Fortunately, Roquefort soon found O'Malley in a side street. When Roquefort told the alley cat about Edgar's wicked tricks, O'Malley's only thought was to try to save Duchess and her kittens.

'My friends will help us!' cried O'Malley. 'They live only a few streets away. Come on, let's go and get them!'

They hurried around to the house where the orchestra had been playing, where Duchess and O'Malley had danced the night away.

'Boys!' cried O'Malley. 'Princess is in danger. We must save her. Follow me!'

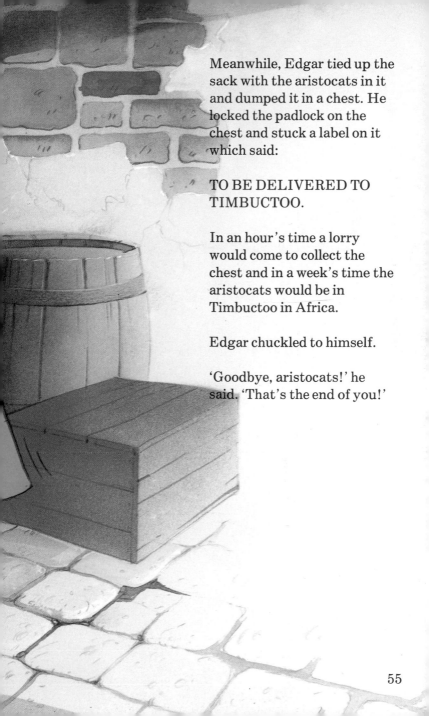

Meanwhile, Edgar tied up the sack with the aristocats in it and dumped it in a chest. He locked the padlock on the chest and stuck a label on it which said:

TO BE DELIVERED TO TIMBUCTOO.

In an hour's time a lorry would come to collect the chest and in a week's time the aristocats would be in Timbuctoo in Africa.

Edgar chuckled to himself.

'Goodbye, aristocats!' he said. 'That's the end of you!'

AAARGH!

Edgar was just pushing the chest towards the front door to await collection when twenty sharp claws dug deeply into his back.

AAARGH! yelled Edgar, rolling over on the floor in agony.

Suddenly, cats seemed to be flying at him from everywhere.

O'Malley's friends tore into Edgar, biting his legs and his arms and scratching his bald head.

As soon as he pushed one of them off, another jumped on to him in its place.

'Leave me alone!' he cried. 'I haven't done anything. I'm Edgar, the faithful servant of madame.'

'We know all about you, Edgar,' cried the cats. And they bit deeper into his flesh.

O'Malley found the key to the chest in Edgar's pocket and undid the padlock.

He took out the sack, bit through the string that tied it, and out popped Duchess and the kittens.

'Oh, Thomas O'Malley!' cried Duchess in delight. 'I knew you could come and rescue us. You're such a *wonderful* creature!'

Meanwhile, O'Malley's friends were bundling Edgar into the chest. They banged the lid on him and locked the padlock.

No one has ever heard a thing from Edgar since he arrived in Timbuctoo.

'Well, I never want to see him again!' declared Madame de Bonnefamille when she returned home and heard what happened.

She was so pleased with O'Malley that she took a photograph of him on the sofa with her aristocats.

'I think he'll make an excellent husband for you, duchess, my dear,' she said.

And Duchess just purred with delight!